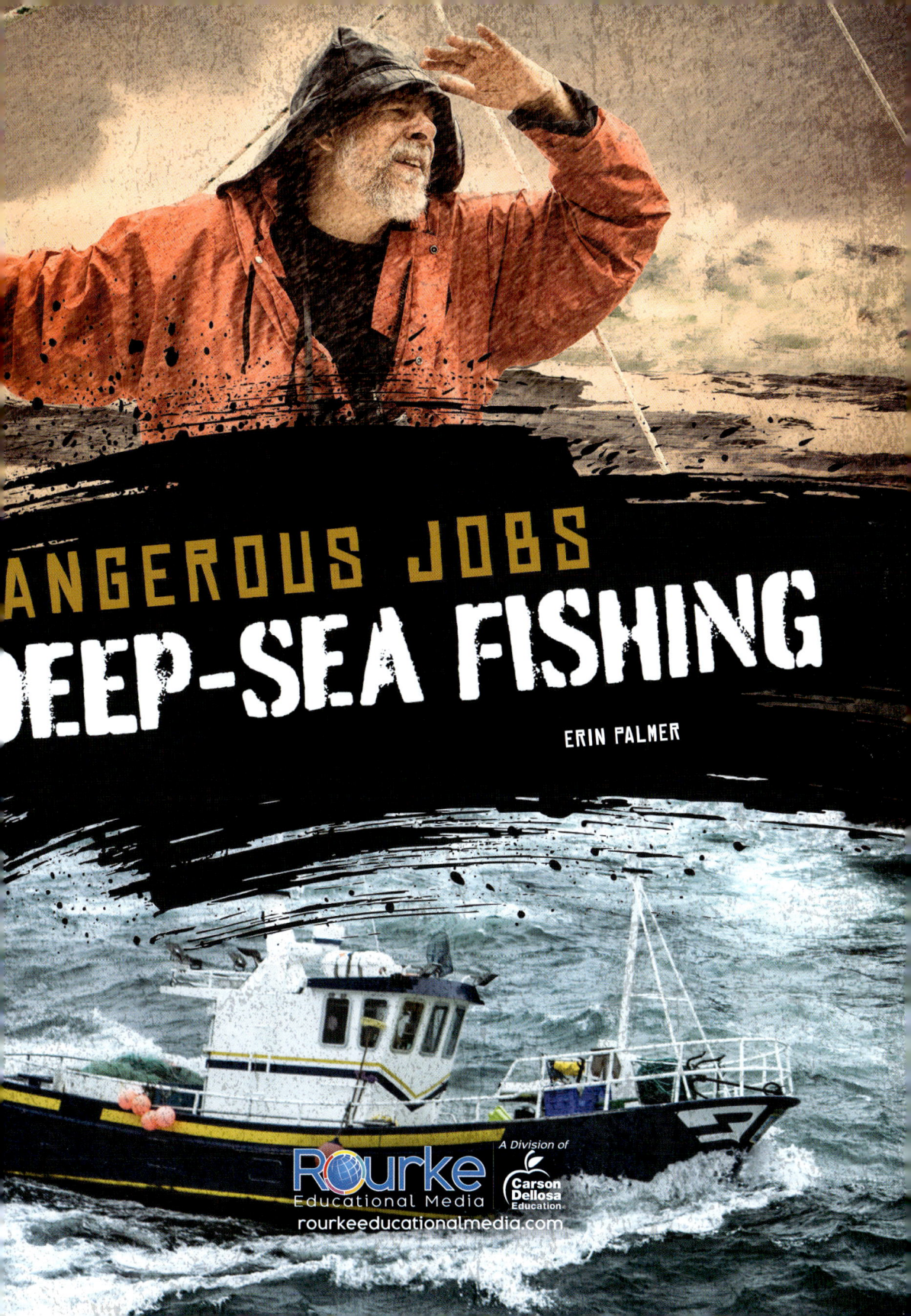

DANGEROUS JOBS
DEEP-SEA FISHING

ERIN PALMER

ROURKE'S SCHOOL to HOME CONNECTIONS
BEFORE AND DURING READING ACTIVITIES

Before Reading: *Building Background Knowledge and Vocabulary*

Building background knowledge can help children process new information and build upon what they already know. Before reading a book, it is important to tap into what children already know about the topic. This will help them develop their vocabulary and increase their reading comprehension.

Questions and Activities to Build Background Knowledge:

1. Look at the front cover of the book and read the title. What do you think this book will be about?
2. What do you already know about this topic?
3. Take a book walk and skim the pages. Look at the table of contents, photographs, captions, and bold words. Did these text features give you any information or predictions about what you will read in this book?

Vocabulary: *Vocabulary Is Key to Reading Comprehension*

Use the following directions to prompt a conversation about each word.

- Read the vocabulary words.
- What comes to mind when you see each word?
- What do you think each word means?

Vocabulary Words:
- affect
- capsize
- deadlier
- gear
- New England
- season

During Reading: *Reading for Meaning and Understanding*

To achieve deep comprehension of a book, children are encouraged to use close reading strategies. During reading, it is important to have children stop and make connections. These connections result in deeper analysis and understanding of a book.

Close Reading a Text

During reading, have children stop and talk about the following:

- Any confusing parts
- Any unknown words
- Text to text, text to self, text to world connections
- The main idea in each chapter or heading

Encourage children to use context clues to determine the meaning of any unknown words. These strategies will help children learn to analyze the text more thoroughly as they read.

When you are finished reading this book, turn to the next-to-last page for **After Reading Questions** and an **Activity**.

Table of Contents

Risky Business 4

Whatever Weather 14

Deadly Coast 25

Memory Game 30

Index 31

After Reading Questions 31

Activity 31

About the Author 32

Risky Business

Sunny days. Salty air. The thrill of the catch. Deep-sea fishing is exciting!

But fishing is dangerous work. Deep-sea fishing is 29 times **deadlier** than most jobs.

Catch Those Critters

A fisher's haul is not just for human food. It is also used for animal feed, bait, and more.

 **deadlier** (DED-lee-ur): more capable of killing

The job does not pay a lot of money. It is a lot of risk for little reward.

gear (geer): equipment or clothing

Broken **gear** can cause problems onboard. Fishers can get tangled in fishing nets.

Fishers work long hours. They often don't have time to sleep! This can **affect** their balance. It can affect their judgment.

affect (uh-FEKT): to change or influence something or someone

Whatever Weather

Fishers catch different fish each **season**. Each type can be found for only a short time.

season (SEE-zuhn): one of the four parts of the year in nature: winter, spring, summer, or fall

The weather can't stop fishers!
They must work rain or shine.

Stormy weather is risky. The boat deck gets slippery. Fishers can be thrown into the water.

"Man overboard!" the crew yells.

Many fishers die after falling overboard. Fishers who die are usually not wearing life vests.

Help, Help!

If the crew doesn't see someone fall, they may not hear their calls for help. It can be noisy at sea!

Boats can **capsize** in any weather. They can sink. Fires can start onboard.

capsize (KAP-size): to turn over in the water

Deadly Disasters
About half of American fishing deaths are caused by boat disasters.

Deadly Coast

America's East Coast is deadly for fishers. In 14 years, 225 fishers died on the job.

A Lot of Loss
The East Coast had the most fisher deaths from 2000 to 2014.

In some **New England** towns, fishing is a way of life. Most residents know a fishing accident victim.

 **New England** (noo ING-gluhnd): a region of the northeastern United States made up of six states: Maine, New Hampshire, Vermont, Massachusetts, Rhode Island, and Connecticut

The Perfect Storm

In 1991, six fishermen vanished during a big storm. They were never found. Their story was told in a book and a movie.

When fishers need help, they call the Coast Guard. Many countries have a Coast Guard. The U.S. Coast Guard is part of the country's military. It enforces laws and protects people at sea.

Memory Game

Look at the pictures. What do you remember reading on the pages where each image appeared?

Index

accident 26
boat(s) 18, 22, 23, 28
Coast Guard 28
East Coast 25
fires 22
money 8
sleep 12
weather 14, 16, 18, 22

After Reading Questions

1. Why is bad weather dangerous for fishers?
2. What part of the United States had the most fisher deaths?
3. Why is it dangerous for fishers to be sleepy?
4. Can a boat catch on fire in the water?
5. What branch of the U.S. military do fishers call for help?

Activity

Imagine you are the captain of a deep-sea fishing vessel. What rules would you have in place to keep your crew safe? Create a poster that lists your on-the-job rules.

About the Author

Erin Palmer is a writer in Tampa, Florida. She loves to travel, try new foods, and go to the beach. Erin has a lot of nieces and nephews, which is why she loves to write books for young people. Her whole huge family loves to read!

© 2020 Rourke Educational Media

All rights reserved. No part of this book may be reproduced or utilized in any form or by any means, electronic or mechanical including photocopying, recording, or by any information storage and retrieval system without permission in writing from the publisher.

www.rourkeeducationalmedia.com

PHOTO CREDITS: Cover and title page: ©Terry J Alcorn (top), Rigel (bottom); p.4-5: ©Zenobillis; p.6-7: ©Kali Nine LLC; p. 8-9, 30: ©sirtravelalot; p.10-11: ©Paolo Cipriani; p.12-13, 30: ©Craig D'Angelo, NOAAWCR; p.14-15: ©ulimi; p.16-17: ©DoublePHOTO studio; p.18-19, 30: © Juan Vilata; p.20: ©Gianluca Fabrizio; p21: ©HadelProductions; p22-23, 30: ©Mr.Lukchai Chaimongkon; p.24, 30: ©Lightguard; p.25: ©designprojects; p.26-27: ©Dan Logan; p.28-29, 30: ©Enjoylife2; p.30-31: ©sharyes17 (background)

Edited by: Kim Thompson
Cover design by: Rhea Magaro-Wallace
Interior design by: Kathy Walsh

Library of Congress PCN Data

Deep-Sea Fishing / Erin Palmer
(Dangerous Jobs)
ISBN 978-1-73161-511-4 (hard cover)
ISBN 978-1-73161-318-9 (soft cover)
ISBN 978-1-73161-616-6 (e-Book)
ISBN 978-1-73161-721-7 (e-Pub)
Library of Congress Control Number: 2019932156

Rourke Educational Media
Printed in the United States of America,
North Mankato, Minnesota